The Book of Days

The Book of Days

National Gallery of Art

Rutledge Books/Galison
Holt, Rinehart and Winston
New York

Cover illustration:
Henri Matisse
Pot of Geraniums
Chester Dale Collection

*Published by Holt, Rinehart and Winston
383 Madison Avenue, New York, New York 10017
Published simultaneously in Canada by
Holt, Rinehart and Winston of Canada, Limited.
ISBN 0-03-052711-2
Printed in Italy by Mondadori, Verona.*

Welcome to the National Gallery of Art *Book of Days,* a combined diary and collection of art reproductions.

As a diary it is unique, for it will never become obsolete. Only month and date are indicated, so you can begin to make entries on any day of the year. *The Book of Days* is as timeless as the art it displays.

As a memento of the Gallery it is very special. It includes seventy-three examples of the masterpieces from this magnificent collection, beautifully reproduced.

Introduction

The collections of the National Gallery of Art, created from the generosity of over four hundred private donors, represent the major schools in Western European art since the thirteenth century and American art from colonial times to the present. Most are the fruits of an American age when prosperity allowed citizens of a young, traditionless country to gather examples from the artistic and cultural traditions of their forebears.

The original structure of the National Gallery of Art, now called the West Building, was the gift to the nation by former Secretary of the Treasury and Ambassador to the Court of St. James, Andrew W. Mellon. During the 1920s Mr. Mellon had begun assembling a collection of fine art with the intention of forming a national gallery in Washington, D.C. His collection of 126 paintings and 26 pieces of sculpture was given to the nation in 1937, the year of his death.

On March 24, 1937, the National Gallery was officially established by a Joint Resolution of Congress. Although formally established as a bureau of the Smithsonian Institution, it is an autonomous organization maintained by the federal government. It is governed by its own board of trustees, members of which include the Chief Justice of the United States, the Secretary of the Smithsonian Institution, and the Secretaries of State and the Treasury, all ex officio, and five distinguished private citizens.

The Gallery's West Building was accepted by President Franklin D. Roosevelt for the people of the United States in 1941. Constructed with funds from the A.W. Mellon Educational and Charitable Trust, it is an impressive neoclassical structure that provides appropriate settings for works by old masters. Its architect was John Russell Pope, who also designed the Jefferson Memorial and the National Archives. The exterior is rose-white Tennessee marble, and the columns in the rotunda were quarried in Tuscany, Italy. Inside, largely native stone decorates the 500,000 square feet of floor space.

Within a generation's time, the National Gallery found it needed to expand. Plans were made to use the trapezoidal plot of land adjacent to the West Building where the Mall and Pennsylvania Avenue converge near the foot of Capitol Hill. The last major undeveloped site on Pennsylvania Avenue, the land had been set aside by Congress in 1937 for the Gallery's future use. Funds for this new building were provided by Paul Mellon and the late Ailsa Mellon Bruce, son and daughter of the donor of the Gallery's West Building, and by The Andrew W. Mellon Foundation.

The location and shape of the site posed several challenges. Located on the inaugural route between the Capitol and the White House, any building constructed there had to be appropriately monumental in scale. The structure also had to abide by the set-back lines established by the National Capital Planning Commission and relate in size to the other buildings along Pennsylvania Avenue and the Mall, especially the Gallery's West Building.

The architects, I. M. Pei and Partners of New York, resolved the problem by cutting the trapezoid into two triangular sections: the larger triangle containing public galleries and the smaller unit housing administrative and curatorial offices and the Center for Advanced Study in the Visual Arts. As a result, the public galleries of the West and East Buildings align on a single axis. And, although boldly different, the contemporary and classical architectural designs are identical in texture and material. In time, the marble facings of the East Building will mellow to the same rose tone of the West.

The East Building was opened on June 1, 1978, to offer a wide variety of art experiences, especially providing for the first time space for contemporary art. "The new building is not a museum of contemporary art," stated the museum's director J. Carter Brown, "but since the National Gallery is an anthology, it cannot stop at any capricious moment in history." The intent is to include definitive modern works so that the progression from medieval times to the present is uninterrupted.

January

James McNeill Whistler
*The White Girl (Symphony in
    White, No. 1)*
Harris Whittemore Collection

1 _____

2 _____

3 _____

4 _____

5 _____

January

Vincent van Gogh
The Olive Orchard
Chester Dale Collection

6

7

8

9

10

January

11

Edouard Vuillard
Child Wearing a Red Scarf
Ailsa Mellon Bruce Collection

12

13

14

15

January

Camille Pissarro
Boulevard des Italiens,
Morning, Sunlight
Chester Dale Collection

16

17

18

19

20

January 21

Jan Vermeer
The Girl with a Red Hat
Andrew W. Mellon Collection

22

23

24

25

January

John Constable
Wivenhoe Park, Essex
Widener Collection

26

27

28

29

30

January
February

Thomas Gainsborough
*Mrs. Richard Brinsley
    Sheridan*
Andrew W. Mellon Collection

31

1

2

3

4

February

William M. Harnett
My Gems
Gift of the Avalon Foundation

5

6

7

8

9

February

Vincent van Gogh
La Mousmé
Chester Dale Collection

10

11

12

13

14

February

L. M. Cooke
Salute to General Washington
in New York Harbor
Gift of Edgar William and
    Bernice Chrysler Garbisch

15

16

17

18

19

February

Georges de La Tour
The Repentant Magdalen
Ailsa Mellon Bruce Fund

20

21

22

23

24

February
March

Claude Monet
Palazzo da Mula, Venice
Chester Dale Collection

25

26

27

28/**29**

1

March

Jan van Eyck
The Annunciation
Andrew W. Mellon Collection

2
_____

3
_____

4
_____

5
_____

6
_____

March

Pierre Bonnard
Two Dogs in a Deserted Street
Ailsa Mellon Bruce Collection

7

8

9

10

11

March

12

Frans Hals
Portrait of an Officer
Andrew W. Mellon Collection

13

14

15

16

March

Henri Matisse
Pot of Geraniums
Chester Dale Collection

17
_____

18
_____

19
_____

20
_____

21
_____

March

Jean-Honoré Fragonard
A Young Girl Reading
Gift of Mrs. Mellon Bruce
  in memory of her father,
  Andrew W. Mellon

22

23

24

25

26

March

Jean-Baptiste-Camille Corot
Forest of Fontainebleau
Chester Dale Collection

27

28

29

30

31

April

Edgar Degas
Four Dancers
Chester Dale Collection

1

2

3

4

5

April

Leonardo da Vinci
Ginevra de'Benci
Ailsa Mellon Bruce Fund

6

7

8

9

10

April

Thomas Eakins
The Biglin Brothers Racing
Gift of Mr. and Mrs. Cornelius
  Vanderbilt Whitney

11

12

13

14

15

April

Giotto
Madonna and Child
Samuel H. Kress Collection

16 _____

17 _____

18 _____

19 _____

20 _____

April

Auguste Renoir
Picking Flowers
Ailsa Mellon Bruce Collection

21

22

23

24

25

April

Rembrandt van Ryn
Portrait of a Lady with an
Ostrich-Feather Fan
Widener Collection

26

27

28

29

30

May

Sassetta and Assistant
*St. Anthony Distributing His
Wealth to the Poor*
Samuel H. Kress Collection

1

2

3

4

5

May

Edouard Manet
The Plum
Collection of Mr. and Mrs.
 Paul Mellon

6

7

8

9

10

May

Amedeo Modigliani
Woman with Red Hair
Chester Dale Collection

11
_____

12
_____

13
_____

14
_____

15
_____

May

Jan Davidsz. de Heem
Vase of Flowers
Andrew W. Mellon Fund

16

17

18

19

20

May

John Sloan
The City from Greenwich Village
Gift of Helen Farr Sloan

21

22

23

24

25

May

Auguste Renoir
Madame Hagen
Gift of Angelika Wertheim Frink

26

27

28

29

30

May
June

31

François Boucher
Allegory of Painting
Samuel H. Kress Collection

1

2

3

4

June

Bartolomé Esteban Murillo
A Girl and Her Duenna
Widener Collection

5

6

7

8

9

June

10

Walt Kuhn
The White Clown
Gift of the W. Averell Harriman
Foundation in memory of
Marie N. Harriman

11

12

13

14

June

Edgar Degas
Mademoiselle Malo
Chester Dale Collection

15

16

17

18

19

June

Peter Paul Rubens
Lion
Ailsa Mellon Bruce Fund

20

21

22

23

24

June

Botticelli
Portrait of a Youth
Andrew W. Mellon Collection

25

_____

26

_____

27

_____

28

_____

29

June
July

30

Joseph Mallord William Turner
*The Junction of the Thames
   and the Medway*
Widener Collection

1

2

3

4

July

Auguste Renoir
Bather Arranging Her Hair
Chester Dale Collection

5

6

7

8

9

July

André Derain
The Old Bridge
Chester Dale Collection

10

_____

11

_____

12

_____

13

_____

14

FRANCOIS · DVC · DALENCON ·
LAGE · DE · XVIII · ANS · LE · XIX ·
IONR · DE · MARS · AN · 1572 ·
FILS · DE · HENRI · II · DE · CE ·
NOM · ROY · DE · FRANCE ·

July

French School
Prince Hercule-François,
Duc d'Alençon
Samuel H. Kress Collection

15
_____

16
_____

17
_____

18
_____

19

July

Gerard ter Borch
The Suitor's Visit
Andrew W. Mellon Collection

20

21

22

23

24

July

Pablo Picasso
The Lovers
Chester Dale Collection

25

26

27

28

29

July
August

Henri Matisse
*Still Life: Apples on Pink
    Tablecloth*
Chester Dale Collection

30

31

1

2

3

August

Berthe Morisot
The Sisters
Gift of Mrs. Charles S.
 Carstairs

4

5

6

7

8

August

Paul Cézanne
House of Père Lacroix
Chester Dale Collection

9

10

11

12

13

August

Mary Cassatt
The Boating Party
Chester Dale Collection

14

15

16

17

18

August

19

Jean-Baptiste-Camille Corot
Ville d'Avray
Gift of Count Cecil Pecci-Blunt

20

21

22

23

August

Henri Rousseau
Boy on the Rocks
Chester Dale Collection

24

25

26

27

28

August
September

Claude Monet
*Woman Seated Under the
Willows*
Chester Dale Collection

29

30

31

1

2

1880 Claude Monet

September

Auguste Renoir
A Girl with a Watering Can
Chester Dale Collection

3

4

5

6

7

September

8

Henri Matisse
Woman with Amphora and
Pomegranates
Ailsa Mellon Bruce Fund

9

10

11

12

September

Jean-Baptiste-Siméon Chardin
The House of Cards
Andrew W. Mellon Collection

13
_____

14
_____

15
_____

16
_____

17
_____

September

18

19

20

21

22

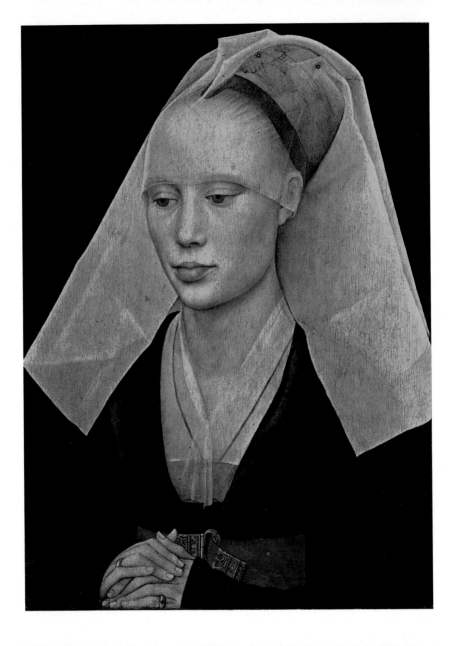

September

23

Rogier van der Weyden
Portrait of a Lady
Andrew W. Mellon Collection

24

25

26

27

September
October

28

Louis Le Nain
Landscape with Peasants
Samuel H. Kress Collection

29

30

1

2

Fatata te Miti   P Gauguin 9[.]

October

Paul Gauguin
Fatata te Miti
Chester Dale Collection

3

4

5

6

7

October

Paul Cézanne
Vase of Flowers
Chester Dale Collection

8

9

10

11

12

October

Gerard David
*The Rest on the Flight into
Egypt*
Andrew W. Mellon Collection

13

14

15

16

17

October

Eugène Boudin
Yacht Basin at
*   Trouville-Deauville*
Ailsa Mellon Bruce Collection

18

19

20

21

22

E. Boudin

les bêtes de la mer...
H. matisse 5o

October

Henri Matisse
Beasts of the Sea
Ailsa Mellon Bruce Fund

23

24

25

26

27

October
November

Hans Holbein the Younger
Edward VI as a Child
Andrew W. Mellon Collection

28

29

30

31

1

PARVVLE PATRISSA, PATRIÆ VIRTVTIS ET HÆRES
ESTO, NIHIL MAIVS MAXIMVS ORBIS HABET.
GNATVM VIX POSSVNT COELVM ET NATVRA DEDISSE,
HVIVS QVEM PATRIS, VICTVS HONORET HONOS.
ÆQVATO TANTVM, TANTI TV FACTA PARENTIS,
VOTA HOMINVM, VIX QVO PROGREDIANTVR, HABENT
VINCITO, VICISTI, QVOT REGES PRISCVS ADORAT
ORBIS, NEC TE QVI VINCERE POSSIT, ERIT.

November

Henri de Toulouse-Lautrec
Quadrille at the Moulin Rouge
Chester Dale Collection

2

3

4

5

6

November

Francesco Guardi
View of the Rialto
Widener Collection

7

8

9

10

11

November

Berthe Morisot
Girl in a Boat with Geese
Ailsa Mellon Bruce Collection

12

13

14

15

16

November

W. H. Brown
Bareback Riders
Gift of Edgar William and
   Bernice Chrysler Garbisch

17

18

19

20

21

November

Claude Monet
The Artist's Garden at Vétheuil
Ailsa Mellon Bruce Collection

22

23

24

25

26

November
December
27

Raphael
St. George and the Dragon
Andrew W. Mellon Collection

28

29

30

1

December

Henri Rousseau
The Equatorial Jungle
Chester Dale Collection

2

3

4

5

6

December

Piet Mondrian
Lozenge in Red, Yellow, and Blue
Gift of Herbert and Nannette Rothschild

7

8

9

10

11

December

Childe Hassam
Allies Day, May 1917
Gift of Ethelyn McKinney in
    memory of her brother,
    Glenn Ford McKinney

12

13

14

15

16

December

Hendrick Avercamp
A Scene on the Ice
Ailsa Mellon Bruce Fund

17

18

19

20

21

December

22

Paul Gauguin
Haystacks in Brittany
Gift of the W. Averell Harriman
  Foundation in memory of
  Marie N. Harriman

23

24

25

26

December

Edgar Degas
Jockey
Gift of Mrs. Jane C. Carey
    for the Addie Burr Clark
    Memorial Collection

27

28

29

30

31

Index

Junction of the Thames and the Medway, The,
   June-July

Kuhn, Walt, June

Landscape with Peasants, September-October
La Tour, Georges de, February
Le Nain, Louis, September-October
Leonardo da Vinci, April
Lion, June
Lovers, The, July
Lozenge in Red, Yellow, and Blue, December

Madame Hagen, May
Mademoiselle Malo, June
Madonna and Child, April
Manet, Edouard, May
Matisse, Henri, March, July-August,
   September, October
Modigliani, Amedeo, May
Mondrian, Piet, December
Monet, Claude, February-March,
   August-September, November
Morisot, Berthe, August, November
Mousmé, La, February
Mrs. Richard Brinsley Sheridan, January-February
Murillo, Bartolomé Esteban, June
My Gems, February

Old Bridge, The, July
Olive Orchard, The, January

Palazzo da Mula, Venice, February-March
Picasso, Pablo, July

Picking Flowers, April
Pissarro, Camille, January
Plum, The, May
Portrait of a Lady, September
Portrait of a Lady with an Ostrich-Feather Fan,
   April
Portrait of an Officer, March
Portrait of a Youth, June
Pot of Geraniums, March
Prince Hercule-François, Duc d'Alençon, July

Quadrille at the Moulin Rouge, November

Raphael, November-December
Rembrandt van Ryn, April
Renoir, Auguste, April, May, July, September
Repentant Magdalen, The, February
Rest on the Flight into Egypt, The, October
Rousseau, Henri, August, December
Rubens, Peter Paul, June

St. Anthony Distributing His Wealth to the Poor,
   May
St. George and the Dragon, November-December
Salute to General Washington in New York Harbor,
   February
Sassetta and Assistant, May
Scene on the Ice, A, December
Sisters, The, August
Sloan, John, May
Still Life: Apples on Pink Tablecloth, July-August
Suitor's Visit, The, July

Ter Borch, Gerard, July

Notes

Notes

Notes